DIS
RL-3
PV-1
ID-7737

The
Littles
and the Trash Tinies

by John Peterson
Pictures by Roberta Carter Clark
Cover illustration by Jacqueline Rogers

A
LITTLE APPLE
PAPERBACK

SCHOLASTIC INC.
New York   Toronto   London   Auckland   Sydney

To Willie and Winnie

ISBN 0-590-46595-3

Text copyright © 1977 by John Peterson.
Illustrations copyright © 1977 by Scholastic Inc.
All rights reserved. Published by Scholastic Inc.
APPLE PAPERBACKS is a registered trademark of Scholastic Inc.

12 11 10 9   7 8/9

Printed in the U.S.A.   **40**

"I don't see any reason why Hildy and Mus Mus can't be friends," said Uncle Nick.

"But Hildy is a cat!" said ten-year-old Tom Little.

"—and Mus Mus is a *mouse*!" said Lucy. She was Tom's eight-year-old sister.

"You know, they might make a great team if we could get them to work together," Tom said.

"What do you mean, Tom?" asked Lucy.

"Mus Mus and Hildy could work together to catch any invading mice," said Tom. "Maybe Mus Mus could lead the mice into a trap." He grinned. " . . . and Hildy could be the trap." Tom snapped his teeth together.

"It's worth a try anyway," said Uncle Nick. "Tom — I'm sure you can control Hildy. And I'll make Mus Mus mind his manners. We ought to try it."

"Fiddlesticks!" said Granny Little. She was sitting in her rocking chair, listening.

"Oh?" said Uncle Nick. He smiled at the old woman. "You don't think it can be done?"

"I don't see the sense in trying it," said Granny Little. She rocked her chair firmly. "We hardly ever have any mice. George Bigg wouldn't stand for it. Besides — putting a cat together with a mouse is like mixing oil with water. It just doesn't work."

"I agree with Granny. It doesn't seem natural to me," said Uncle Pete from the other side of the room. He got up from his favorite chair by the fireplace and limped over to where the others were talking. "Cats and mice are enemies: always have been." He shook his head. "They're natural born enemies."

Suddenly Aunt Lily stepped into the room. She was holding a steaming cake pan. "This year's first fruitcake!" she announced. "Smell that!" Aunt Lily waved the fruitcake under Granny Little's nose.

The old lady took a deep breath. "Umm—delicious!"

"May I have a piece, Aunt Lily?" asked Lucy.

"My stars!" Aunt Lily said. "My first fruitcake of the Christmas season, and already there are hungry Littles waiting to eat it all up. Why, I used *one* whole cherry and *one* walnut in this cake." She laughed. "No, Lucy — you may not have a piece. I'm going to make four more of these before I'm through. And *no one* is going to get a bite until Christmas day." She turned on her heel and walked into the kitchen.

"Well, Lily is here," said Uncle Pete. "That's plain to see. And she's as bossy as ever."

"She's super!" said Lucy. "Christmas is the best holiday there is because Aunt Lily comes to stay for two whole weeks."

Mrs. Little entered the room. She was carrying Baby Betsy. "Heaven knows we'd have a skimpy Christmas around here without Aunt Lily," she said. Then she sighed. "She does *everything!*"

The Littles were tiny people. They were so tiny that a cherry looked as

big as a pumpkin to them. And a
pumpkin was big enough for the entire
family to hide behind. Or—if it was
hollowed out—to stand in!

Why were the Littles so tiny? They
were born tiny. As far as any of them
knew, there had always been tiny
people living in the world. There was
nothing in the history books about tiny
people. That was because history books
were written by big people and they
didn't even know that tiny people
existed.

Nevertheless, all tiny people knew
that some of their ancestors were in
Philadelphia when the Declaration of
Independence was signed. And they

were at Gettysburg when the great battle of the Civil War was fought.

Sometimes tiny people helped. Take the famous ride of Paul Revere, for example. There were *two* lanterns hung in the tower of the Old North Church to warn that the British were moving by boat. One of the lanterns went out right after it was hung up. It wasn't noticed — except by a tiny person who lived in the church. He quickly relit the second lantern and the right message got through.

There was one other thing about the tiny people that was different. They had tails! If the Littles thought about their tails at all it was to wonder why *they* were lucky enough to be born with them while big people were not.

The Littles took their tails for granted. And they carried them high when they were in good spirits, which was most of the time.

All the Littles except Aunt Lily lived in a ten-room apartment in the walls of a house owned by Mr. George Bigg. Mr. Bigg, his wife, and their son, Henry, didn't know anything about the Littles or their apartment. They had never seen a Little. They had never even seen a clue that would make them think there were tiny people living with them in the same house.

The Biggs's cat, Hildy, knew the Littles very well however. Tom Little had made friends with the cat some time ago. Since then she had taken part in many of their adventures — including the time she helped rescue Aunt Lily in a snowstorm.

Aunt Lily lived in Doctor Zigger's house, four houses away from the Biggs. By secretly watching the doctor and reading his old medical books in the attic, she had learned to be a nurse.

"I'm *so* glad that Aunt Lily is here," said Lucy. "But when will Cousin Dinky and Della get here? We can't have Christmas without *them*!"

Mrs. Little sighed. She hugged Baby Betsy. "I'm worried about that," she said.

Granny Little spoke: "There's plenty of time for them to make it," she said. "The snowstorm will be over. The weather man said probably tomorrow."

"*Probably!*" Uncle Pete said. "Umph! Why don't they know? They've got satellites going around the earth taking weather pictures. They've got all sorts of gadgets and ways to find out."

"What about your leg, Uncle Pete?" asked Tom. He grinned and winked at Lucy. "What does your leg say about the storm?"

Uncle Pete slapped his leg. He had been wounded in the Mouse Invasion of '34, and walked with a limp since that time. "This old leg of mine always hurts a bit when there's a storm. Yessir! I can feel that storm. It's a big one."

Uncle Nick laughed. "Only trouble is—it begins to hurt *after* the storm has already started. It doesn't tell you a thing you don't already know."

Uncle Pete nodded. "Right!" he said. He stood up, picked up his cane, and limped to the fireplace. "And the doggone leg keeps on hurting for a day after the storm is over." He shoved a twig into the fireplace and stood there watching it until the fire flamed up.

Just then Mr. William T. Little came into the room.

"Dad," said Tom. "You're covered with snow."

Lucy brushed her father off.

"It's wild up there," said Mr. Little. He had been on the roof. "Dinky and Della will never fly in that storm."

"Cousin Dinky can fly in any kind of weather," said Lucy. "He told me so."

"*And* he's lost a few gliders doing it," said Mr. Little.

"Dinky isn't going to do anything foolish," said Granny Little. She drew her shawl over her shoulders and rocked in her chair. "There's plenty of time. He won't take a chance he doesn't have to."

"Oh, I hope you're right," Mrs. Little said.

"Christmas isn't until next week," Granny Little went on. "Dinky and his darling wife can just stay where they are until Peter's leg feels better."

"Mother! Daddy! Come quickly! *Everyone* come!" It was Lucy yelling. She ran into the apartment.

"Something terrible has happened to Uncle Nick!"

"I knew it!" Granny Little said. "I knew that cat and mouse experiment wouldn't work."

All the Littles followed Lucy into the wall passageway. Aunt Lily stopped long enough to pick up her nurse's bag.

"Where is he, Lucy?" cried Mr. Little.

"In the attic," said Lucy. "Oh, Daddy! Uncle Nick is hurt really bad. I know it."

They got to the attic. Tom was bending over Uncle Nick, who looked very pale.

Hildy, the cat, was sitting nearby, licking her paw.

The Littles crowded around Uncle Nick.

"Stand back, everyone," said Aunt Lily. "Give me room to look at him."

"He's hardly breathing," Tom said. "And he feels cold."

"Will Uncle Nick die?" whispered Lucy.

"Shhh!" said Mrs. Little.

"Nick is in shock," announced Aunt Lily.

"Will someone get a blanket or something to cover him? Tom — help me raise his feet." Aunt Lily looked around. "Get that pencil over there."

She pointed. "We can put his feet on that."

In a few moments Uncle Nick was covered and his feet were raised. He was mumbling.

Uncle Pete leaned closer. "What's he saying?"

"He's dazed," Aunt Lily said. "He doesn't know what's going on."

Later, after Uncle Nick was back in the apartment and in bed, Mr. Little had some questions: "What happened, Tom?" he said. "What's this about a cat and mouse experiment?"

"We were trying to see if Hildy and Mus Mus could be friends," said Tom. He shook his head. "I guess they can't."

"Tell him what Hildy did, Tom," said Lucy.

"She just went cuckoo," Tom said. "I couldn't stop her. She went right after Mus Mus. And I guess she would have killed him — but Uncle Nick jumped in between them."

"In between a *cat* and a *mouse*?" said Uncle Pete.

Tom nodded. "Hildy was charging so fast she wouldn't have been able to stop if she wanted to."

"And — ?" said Mr. Little.

"She knocked Uncle Nick right over," Tom said. "She *stepped* on him, I think."

"Oh dear," said Mrs. Little. "That heavy cat, oh dear!"

"He'll be all right," Uncle Pete said. "Don't worry. It'll take more than that to do in Nick." He looked around at everyone. "Why, he spent *thirty* years fighting mice in the city dump. He's been chased, surrounded, and done-for a hundred times and he's always come through. Why—one of those beasts even bit off his tail!" He looked toward the bedroom where Uncle Nick was lying. "He's had to wear a *false* tail— think of it!"

"This was a *cat*, Peter," said Granny Little. "Not a mouse."

"I should have been able to stop Hildy," said Tom. "It's my fault."

"That's not true, Tom," said Mr. Little. "Your Uncle Nick is a grown man. He knew what he was doing when he stepped in front of Hildy. You can't blame yourself."

"It was his choice," Mr. Little went on, "to save his mouse."

"He risked his life to save a mouse," said Uncle Pete. "Can you imagine that? A *mouse!*"

"A very special mouse," Mr. Little said. "A mouse he had trained to find other mice. A soldier-mouse that could take him safely in and out of Trash City in the town dump — a place, as you know, that is completely surrounded by enemy mice at all times. Mus Mus was comrade-in-arms, a companion, and a friend to Nick."

"He loves Mus Mus," Lucy said.

Uncle Pete looked toward Uncle Nick's room. "Here comes Lily," he said. "Now we'll see how bad it is."

Aunt Lily came into the room. She spoke in a hushed voice. "He's going to be all right," she said. "He's got bruises all over his body, but he's going to be all right — there's nothing broken, I think."

"I'm glad," said Mr. Little.

"Thank goodness!" Granny Little said.

"But we do have a big problem," said Aunt Lily. She tiptoed back and closed the door to Uncle Nick's room. "He was so badly scared and he hurts all over so much—he's *sure* he's dying!"

"Fiddlesticks!" said Granny Little. "He's a big baby, that's why he's making a fuss."

"Well, that may be true," said Aunt Lily, "but it's still a problem. Nick thinks he's dying. He wants to see some of his friends from Trash City before he dies."

"He can't travel to the town dump in his condition, can he?" asked Mr. Little.

"Certainly not!" Aunt Lily said. "He may not be dying, but he has been badly bruised. Right now he couldn't walk if he wanted to."

"Christmas is coming," said Mrs. Little. "He misses his friends. We should send for them: they should come *here*. It would be the best Christmas present we could give him."

"There's a snowstorm," said Mr. Little.

"The storm will stop soon, won't it?" asked Mrs. Little.

Aunt Lily turned to walk from the room. "He's calling me," she said.

"Poor Lily," said Mrs. Little. "She has been working so very hard on Christmas, and now this."

Uncle Pete limped back and forth. "If only there was some way we could get Nick's friends here to cheer him up."

Suddenly Tom leaped from his chair. "I have it!" he shouted. "I have an idea!"

"Tom!" said Uncle Pete. "Don't get so excited. Have some respect for your wounded uncle."

"Let the boy be," said Granny Little. "Children have to jump up and down. They're made that way."

"Let's hear your idea, Tom," said Mr. Little. "We sure could use one."

"The snowstorm won't bother us too much," Tom said, "if we go to the dump on the garbage truck—just hitchhike a ride!"

"Garbage truck?" said Mrs. Little. "Oh dear, no!"

"Tom's right," Granny Little said. "It's so simple I wonder why we didn't think of it before."

Mr. Little sat nodding his head. "It could be done," he said. "While the trash-man is picking up the Biggs's garbage some of us could sneak aboard his truck." Mr. Little turned to Tom. "When do they pick up the garbage?"

"This afternoon," Tom said.

"Then we're in luck," said Mr. Little. "And when does the truck return?"

"Friday afternoon," said Tom.

"How would you find anyone in that dump?" asked Granny Little. "The place where the Tinies live is hidden, isn't it?"

"Yes," said Mr. Little. "I suppose it would be like looking for a needle in a haystack. If only Dinky were here. He knows the place."

"Good!" Mrs. Little said. She sat back in the sofa. "You're not going." She looked around at everybody. "I mean, I'm sorry for Uncle Nick's sake you won't be able to go. But I'm glad you won't be going on that garbage truck to that awful dump."

"Mus Mus knows the way," said Lucy.

"Of course!" said Mr. Little. "Lucy's right."

"*I* could get Mus Mus to lead us to Trash City, once we get to the dump," said Lucy proudly.

"She can!" said Tom. "Mus Mus likes Lucy. For some reason he takes orders from Lucy and he won't from me. It's weird."

"*Tom*—it's not *weird*," said Mrs. Little. She smiled at her daughter. "Lucy has a talent with mice." Then she added, "But I don't think you should trust a mouse and a little girl to get you there. My goodness!"

Mr. Little put his arm around Mrs. Little. "Lucy will be all right," he said. "She's smart and she won't take chances. Besides, I'll be with her every step of the way."

"I'll go too," Tom said.

"If you think she'll be safe," said Mrs. Little. She looked at her husband and nodded her head. "I know it should be done . . . for Uncle Nick."

"I'll stay here," Uncle Pete said. "I'll try to keep the old soldier from getting too depressed."

"All this fuss over Nick!" said Granny Little. "I declare—he has a wonderful family. I hope he knows it."

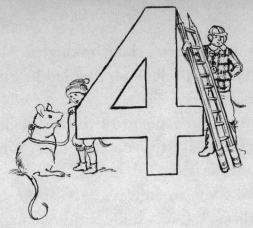

That afternoon Mr. Little, Tom, and Lucy hid behind a telephone pole. It was near the Biggs's garbage cans. Lucy held the leash of Uncle Nick's white mouse, Mus Mus. Mr. Little held a ladder made from two pencils and some match sticks. The snow was still falling.

"If we get much more of this snow," Mr. Little said, "we won't be able to get to the truck when it comes."

"The garbage man usually parks right near this telephone pole," said Tom. "All we have to do is put the ladder up against the running board of the truck."

"I sure hope it's long enough," Mr. Little said. He looked the ladder up and down.

"The running board of the truck has an extra small step down," said Tom. "It'll work."

"Tom — you're always so *sure* of everything," Lucy said, "and when it doesn't work —"

Just then a large blue-and-white garbage truck turned the nearby corner and headed their way.

"This is it!" said Mr. Little. "Good luck to all of us!"

They crouched behind the telephone pole. Lucy shivered.

"Don't be afraid, Lucy," said Tom.

"I'm not afraid," Lucy said. "I'm cold."

The garbage truck came to a halt exactly where Tom said it would. The motor kept on running. The door swung open and a man came down the two steps to the street. He left the door open.

The man walked quickly over to the Biggs's garbage cans. He began to carry them to the back of his truck.

"*Now!*" whispered Mr. Little. He stepped from behind the telephone pole and propped the ladder against the small step beneath the running board. It fit perfectly.

"See," Tom said. He looked at Lucy. "I told you."

The three tiny people and the mouse climbed the ladder quickly. Mr. Little and Tom pulled the ladder up behind them. They placed it against the next step and everyone climbed up to that one too.

"One more," said Mr. Little. He was breathing heavily. This time he placed the ladder against the truck's body near the open door. The tiny people scurried up the ladder and into the cab of the truck.

"Over here!" cried Tom. "Here's a place to hide where the driver won't see us." He pointed under the seat.

Mr. Little and Lucy followed Tom into the hiding place.

In a few moments the garbage truck went to work grinding up the Biggs's garbage. It was being compressed into the back of the truck.

The garbage man climbed into the cab. He shifted gears and the truck went down the road.

It was a long bumpy trip.

The garbage truck stopped at all the houses between the Biggs's house and the town dump. Stop! Go! Stop! Go!

There was the steady noisy clatter of the machine that pressed the garbage into the back of the truck. Tom and Lucy huddled under the seat in the truck's cab. Whenever the door was open, icy cold air blew in on them. When the door was closed, the truck's heater blasted hot air.

Tom checked and rechecked his pack. He wondered if he had brought enough arrows for his bow. Lucy kept whispering to Mus Mus whenever the man was out of the truck.

Mr. Little worried out loud: "It's getting dark. We're going to get there when it's dark."

Tom searched his memory: he was trying to think of all the things Uncle Nick had said about the dump.

Finally, the smell of burning garbage! It was the dump. There were shouts of men working. The truck swung around and backed up. They were unloading the truck.

"Let's get out of here," said Mr. Little. He stood in the truck door.

"The ladder, Dad!" said Tom. "We'll need it to get back."

They got the ladder from under the seat.

"Hurry!" Lucy said.

Mr. Little tossed the ladder into a snowbank. It disappeared beneath the snow.

"Jump!" commanded Mr. Little. "Jump near the ladder. Stay hidden in the snow until the truck leaves."

Mr. Little and Tom jumped.

Lucy got a good grip on the mouse's leash. She threw herself into space, pulling Mus Mus with her. They tumbled head over heels for two long feet.

The fluffy white snow softened Lucy's landing. The tiny girl stuck her head out of the snowbank. She saw Tom's head. He was looking back at her from a few feet away.

Tom put his fingers to his lips. "Shhh!" he said. Then he ducked back under the snow.

After a while the truck drove away. It was now 5:30, the end of the working day. The rest of the men left too. The Littles were alone in the town dump.

"Well, well," Mr. Little said as he dug himself out of the snow, "that wasn't any fun. Where is everybody?"

The children popped out of the snow.

"Here!" said Tom.

They brushed each other off. Mus Mus shook himself, then combed his whiskers with his front paws.

"Let's see," said Mr. Little, thinking out loud. "It's dark. It's cold. I'm hungry. We don't have any idea where we are."

"Mus Mus knows," Lucy said.

"Well, anyhow," said Mr. Little, "I think we'll spend the night near here and look for Trash City first thing in the morning." He looked around. "I don't want to go prowling about in a strange place at night."

"Where shall we make our camp?" asked Tom.

Mr. Little led them over piles of trash. They came to one of the many small fires burning in the dump.

"If we keep close to one of these fires," he said, "we can stay warm."

"And animals will stay away too," Lucy said. "They're afraid of fire."

The Littles began preparing their camp site. They all carried plastic sandwich bags in their packs. They had taken them from Mrs. Biggs's kitchen.

Mr. Little spread one of the plastic bags on the snow. He placed it near the fire. "This is our ground cloth," he said. "There's as much cold under us as there is in the air, maybe more. It's important to have as much protection under us as it is to have it on top of us."

Mr. Little placed the second sandwich bag on top of the ground cloth. He got out their sleeping bag: it was made from one of Mr. Biggs's woolen socks—about six inches of the sock from the toe back toward the heel. Mr. Little stuffed the sock into the second sandwich bag. Finally, he and Tom made a lean-to out of the last two sandwich bags and some twigs.

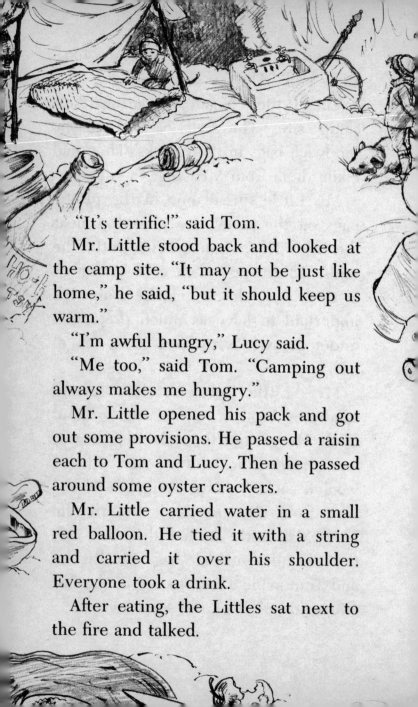

"It's terrific!" said Tom.

Mr. Little stood back and looked at the camp site. "It may not be just like home," he said, "but it should keep us warm."

"I'm awful hungry," Lucy said.

"Me too," said Tom. "Camping out always makes me hungry."

Mr. Little opened his pack and got out some provisions. He passed a raisin each to Tom and Lucy. Then he passed around some oyster crackers.

Mr. Little carried water in a small red balloon. He tied it with a string and carried it over his shoulder. Everyone took a drink.

After eating, the Littles sat next to the fire and talked.

"I still don't understand why Uncle Nick thinks he's dying," said Lucy.

"It's kind of hard to explain, Lucy," said Mr. Little. "Older people think about these things more than younger people, probably."

"I *never* think about dying," said Tom. "That's dumb."

"Uncle Nick isn't dumb, Tom," said Lucy. "Is he, Daddy?"

Mr. Little shook his head "no."

Lucy looked up at her father. "You won't die, will you, Daddy?"

Mr. Little smiled. "Not one day soon," he said. "I hope not anyway."

"I don't think we should worry about it," Tom said.

"I'm not *awful* worried about it," said Lucy. She moved closer to her father.

Mr. Little put his arm around Lucy. "When we bring Uncle Nick's friends to see him," he said, "he'll probably feel better about everything."

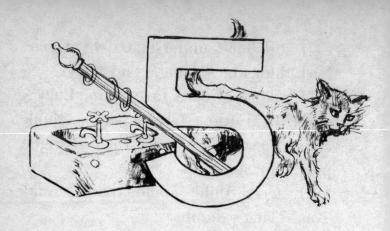

"Daddy, wake up!" Lucy whispered.

"Wh—at?" Mr. Little rubbed his eyes.

"There's a mean-looking yellow cat in that pile of junk over there!"

Mr. Little looked around in the early morning light. "Does it see us?"

"I don't think so," whispered Lucy.

Mr. Little poked Tom. "Wake up, Tom!"

Tom began to speak. His father put a hand over the boy's mouth. "Cat!" he said.

Tom's eyes widened.

As silently as possible the Littles climbed out of their sleeping bag. Without speaking they went to work taking down the lean-to. They folded the sandwich bags. Everything was put away. They picked up their packs and swung them over their shoulders.

"I don't see that mean cat anymore," Lucy whispered.

Uncle Nick's white mouse was pacing back and forth. He tugged at his leash.

"Let Mus Mus go, Lucy," said Mr. Little. "He'll lead us away from that cat."

When the mouse was let go he began to run. The Littles scrambled after him. They tried not to make any noise.

Mus Mus led the Littles deep into the dump. They cli   l over piles of tin cans and broken   'es, passed a smashed automobile, a.   went under a tall dresser with a broken mirror.

Suddenly the mouse darted into the end of a pipe. The opening was about four inches across. The pipe stuck out of the trash at an angle.

The three Littles jumped into the pipe after the white mouse.

Snow had fallen into the pipe and drifted down the length of it. Over the last few days of the storm the snow melted and froze into ice.

The Littles slipped on the ice and fell down inside the pipe. They tried to get to their feet. They slipped and slid. Down, down they went, sliding deeper and deeper into the junk pile.

"Stay together!" yelled Mr. Little. He and his children were sliding down a pipe into the middle of the junk pile.

Mr. Little tried to grab Tom and Lucy, but he couldn't. They were sliding away from him.

At last, one by one, they shot out of the end of the pipe. The three of them piled up in a heap.

"Where are we?" asked Mr. Little. He stood up and looked around.

"We're *under* the junk!" Tom said.

"Then this must be Trash City," said Mr. Little.

"There goes Mus Mus!" yelled Lucy. She ran after the mouse.

Mr. Little and Tom caught up with Lucy. She was standing near a tiny girl as tall as she was. The girl was petting Mus Mus. She wore a dress that was spotted with colorful patches. "I saw you with Mus Mus," she said. "What have you done with old Major Nick?"

In a few moments more tiny people appeared. They came from behind soup cans, milk bottles, broken barrels, and other kinds of trash. Their clothing was worn and patched too.

A man with a bushy red beard and a black patch over his eye stepped forward.

"Who are you?" he called out.

"I'm William T. Little," said Mr. Little, "and these are my children — Tom and Lucy."

The man with the eye patch turned to a tall, long-faced man: "Did he say Little?"

The tall man nodded. "Yep!"

Mr. Little smiled. He held out his arms and crossed them. (He was following Uncle Nick's instructions.) "We're relatives of Nick Little," he said. Then: "*Major* Nicholas Q. Little, retired . . . of the Mouse Force Brigade . . . here, in Trash City."

"You're kin of Major Nick?" asked the man with the eye patch.

"He's our *uncle!*" said Lucy proudly.

The man broke into a big smile. He walked toward the Littles with his arms crossed and held out. "I'm Itsy Clutter," he said. "I'm the mayor of this here town. Welcome to Trash City."

Mr. Little and Mayor Clutter greeted each other. They did it in the manner of the people of Trash City: they crossed their arms and shook both hands at the same time.

Mr. Little explained why he and his children had come to Trash City. He told how they found their way by following Mus Mus. He said that Uncle Nick wanted very much to see some of his friends for Christmas.

Mayor Clutter and the Trash Tinies were happy to do anything for Major Nick Little. The old soldier was well liked by the people of the strange city under the trash.

"You'll want to start back as soon as you can," said the mayor. "I'll take you to Major Nick's friends. I'm sure they'll be pleased to go with you."

Mr. Little told Mayor Clutter how they had traveled to the town dump. "The garbage truck goes back to the

Biggs's house day after tomorrow," he said, "and because of the snowstorm we have no other way to get back there. I'm afraid we'll have to spend a few days with you."

"Wonderful!" Mayor Clutter said. "You are welcome to stay in my orange crate."

"Orange crate?" said Tom.

"That's right, Tom," said Mayor Clutter. "Here in the town dump we make our homes out of the trash and broken furniture."

"Golly," said Lucy. "That sounds like fun."

They started out for Mayor Clutter's home. On the way he pointed out where other Trash Tinies lived. The Ash family lived in a barrel; the Orts lived under a table in a chest of drawers; the Rummages lived in a steamer trunk.

"The Rummages are a very large

family," Mayor Clutter explained. "That is why they have one of the bigger homes."

They passed a bathtub. "This is our Community Youth Center," said the mayor. "The children swim in the tub when the weather is warm. Right now they are skating on the ice."

Lucy pointed to a broken bicycle. "Look, Tom!" she yelled. "The kids have a Ferris wheel." Tom saw a group of tiny children. They were swinging

up and around on a spinning bicycle tire.

"I see that the houses have electric lights," said Mr. Little. "How do you manage that?"

"We use strings of old Christmas tree lights," said Mayor Clutter. "The electric power comes from used automobile batteries. You would be amazed how many useful things big people throw away. They are very, very wasteful."

"Lucky for tiny people," said Mr. Little.

"We live very comfortably," Mayor Clutter added.

"I'm surprised, I must say," said Mr. Little. "I thought since you lived in the town dump you must be quite ..."

"Poor?" said the mayor. Mayor Clutter laughed. "You will see that we have everything we need and more."

Tom spoke: "But ... the patches on your clothes?"

Mayor Clutter laughed again. "That's the *style*, Tom," he said. "Trash Tinies love the patched look."

They came to a five-drawer metal filing cabinet. "This is an apartment house," said Mayor Clutter. "The Scrap family, the Wastes, the Dregs, and the Raggs live here."

Mr. Little looked over his head. "I don't understand," he said. "Why doesn't all this overhead junk just fall down on you?"

The mayor smiled. "It's quite an engineering job, I can tell you," he said. "It does *look* like a pile of junk. After all, we don't want any big people to think there are tiny people living here. Actually, the roof of Trash City is very well supported. There are large metal braces, pipes, and storage tanks. And they are all locked together in such a way as to be terrifically strong."

"What happens when it rains?" asked Mr. Little. "Doesn't the water seep down and give you problems?"

"The water is handled by a system of pipes, old gutters, and tubs," Mayor Clutter replied. "We keep what water we need, and the rest is drained off into the ground."

"This is remarkable," Mr. Little said. "I had no idea that you had solved all these problems. I'm very impressed."

They came at last to Mayor Clutter's home in the orange crate.

Mayor Clutter introduced the Littles to his family. First, there was Mrs. Clutter whom he called "Mrs. C." Next there were the two boys, Jum, who was Tom's age, and Spunk, a year younger. A girl, Cubby, who was fifteen, was on an errand.

The Clutters were told the news about "Major Nick."

"I'm sorry to hear the old Major is laid up and feeling poorly," said Mrs. Clutter. "We were hoping he'd spend Christmas with us."

"What's for breakfast, Mrs. C.?" asked Mayor Clutter. "Our friends are hungry after their long trip."

"It's not here yet, my dear," said Mrs. Clutter. "Cubby went to fetch it just before you got home."

"Then you don't cook?" asked Mr. Little.

"Oh, my dear — no," Mrs. Clutter said. "We just send one of the young 'uns over to the community kitchen for the food."

"Here she comes now," said Mayor Clutter.

Fifteen-year-old Cubby Clutter came into the orange crate. She was carrying a bowl of steaming food.

"What did we get this time, Cubby dear?" asked Mrs. Clutter.

Cubby made a face. "It's chicken-noodle soup," she said. "We *never* get what I want."

"Do you like chicken-noodle soup, Mr. Little?" asked Mayor Clutter.

"For breakfast?" said Tom.

"Tom!" said Mr. Little. He looked sternly at the boy. He turned to Mayor

49

Clutter. "Some piping hot chicken-noodle soup would hit the spot right now," he said. "We'll eat whatever you have and enjoy it."

"Well, that's more than I can say about the Clutters," said the mayor. "We eat what they give us but we don't always like it. But it's the system, so we try not to complain."

"The system?" said Mr. Little.

"Major Nick didn't tell you about the system?"

"Major Nick, it seems, has told us precious little about Trash City," said Mr. Little. "Most of his stories had to do with fighting mice."

"Well now—where do you think we get our food, Mr. Little?" asked Mayor Clutter.

"Come to think of it, I don't know," Mr. Little said. "You don't have some amazing way of farming down here, do you?"

Mayor Clutter shook his head.

"—and there aren't any big people to get leftovers from," Lucy said.

"—and no woods or fields where wild food grows," Tom said.

Lucy made a face. "You don't," she said quietly, "... you don't eat ... gar—" She couldn't finish.

"GARBAGE?" roared Mayor Clutter. He laughed until tears came to his eyes. "Oh no, Lucy! No! No! No! My goodness, what an idea."

Lucy blushed. "Well ... I thought— it *is* the town dump!" she said.

"Lucy!" said Mr. Little. He shook his finger at Lucy.

"No, Lucy," Mayor Clutter went on, "the garbage is thrown away in another part of the dump. It's burned every day." He raised his eyebrows and wrinkled his nose. "Sometimes when the wind is blowing the wrong way we get a kind of smelly pollution."

51

By this time everyone was eating the hot soup.

Tom stopped eating. "Then where do you get the food, Mayor Clutter?" he asked.

The mayor smiled. "You can go on eating, Tom," he said. "The food is perfectly safe. It's *canned* food. It comes from a nearby supermarket."

"Do you take it from the store?" asked Mr. Little.

"No—they throw it away," said Mayor Clutter. "A certain number of cans in the store lose their paper labels for one reason or another. The store people forget what is in the cans. They can't sell 'em, so they throw them in the garbage."

"And you get them," added Tom.

"That's right," said Mayor Clutter. "We don't know what is in the cans either, so we open them up one by one. Whatever we find, we eat. And that's why sometimes we have food for breakfast that would be better for lunch. And we may get something for dinner that would be better for breakfast."

"Then *everybody* in Trash City will be eating chicken-noodle soup for breakfast today?" said Mr. Little.

"That's right," said the mayor.

"It's good food," Mrs. Clutter said.

"Once we got *three* cans of peas in a row!" said Spunk, the youngest Clutter.

"Yuk!" said his brother.

"Double yuk!" said Cubby.

Everybody laughed.

After breakfast Mayor Clutter led the Littles through the streets of Trash City. They were on their way to meet Uncle Nick's friends. Wherever they walked, people came out to meet them. Everyone had a kind word to say about "old Major Nick."

Suddenly they heard an automobile horn.

The people in the streets began running every which way.

"What is it?" asked Mr. Little.

"Mouse alert!" yelled Mayor Clutter. "Follow me!" He ran off.

The mayor led the Littles to a

stepladder in the center of the city. It was the highest place around. The steps of the ladder were broken: it, too, was a piece of trash.

Underneath the ladder was an empty fruit-cocktail can. The mayor climbed into the can. "Get in!" he said to the Littles. "This is our tower elevator."

Sure enough—the can was the cab of an elevator. It was raised and lowered by means of a pulley system and some string. They started up.

"We have a tin-can elevator like this at home," Tom told Mayor Clutter.

The mayor nodded. "Your uncle helped us make this one, Tom," he said.

The top step of the ladder helped support the ceiling of trash. Hanging below the top step was a cigar box. "This is our observation platform," said Mayor Clutter. "We can see the entire town from here."

The tin-can elevator stopped at the cigar box. Everyone climbed out.

Mayor Clutter went quickly to a large pair of binoculars. They were hanging from the top step of the ladder. One lens was broken. The mayor looked through the other lens with his good eye. He turned the binoculars right and left, looking at the city below.

Finally he said: "I don't see a battle going on anywhere." Then he picked up a small hammer. "I'll send a signal to see if anyone is fighting mice." A bell was hanging nearby. The mayor hit it with the hammer.

Almost at once an answer came from below. Whistles and drums were heard from different parts of the city.

"They are signaling back to tell me they don't see any mice," the mayor explained. "It was a false alarm. We get them now and then."

"No mice?" said Mr. Little.

"I'm glad," Lucy said.

"Aw gee!" said Tom.

"We are *always* expecting an attack," said the mayor. "I don't mind a false alarm. It gives us a chance to see how fast we can get to our stations and to check our equipment."

"Everyone has a place to go then?" asked Mr. Little.

"Oh yes," said the mayor. He pointed. "See those people over at the far end of the city? They are in charge of a Mouse Force Battery of aerosol bombs. They're for killing insects, but mice hate to be squirted with the stuff. The cans can be rolled to any place. From up here I can see all of the battlefield. By using the bell I can signal to those below to take the bombs where they are needed."

The mayor pointed to another group of tiny people. They were standing near a bathtub. "In case we are losing the battle, our people can be signaled to go to the high places in the city," he said. "Those people near the bathtub will pull the plug and all the water in that tub will flood the low-lying places."

"What a neat plan!" Tom said.

"What do you do with the children and the old people during a battle?" asked Mr. Little.

"They go to special forts surrounded by mouse traps," said Mayor Clutter.

"You've thought of everything," said Mr. Little.

"We have to be well organized to defend our way of life," said the mayor. "The mice in this dump could wipe us out."

The tiny people took the tin-can elevator down. They walked through the streets of Trash City. Mayor Clutter pointed out interesting buildings. He introduced the Littles to more of the town's citizens.

Soon they came to a bunch of rusty tin cans. They were arranged in the shape of a building: small cans were piled on top of large ones. At the bottom was an upside-down washtub. There was a doorway cut into the side of the tub. Over the door a sign read:

TRASH CITY
HOME FOR
CHILDREN

Mayor Clutter knocked on the door.

In a few moments an old man came to the door. "Howdy, mayor," he said.

"This is Mr. Lars T. Penny," said Mayor Clutter. "He's the father, mother, nurse, big brother, and warm friend of all the homeless children who live in Trash City."

"Homeless!" Tom said. "Do you mean there are children without parents in Trash City?" he asked.

"Yes, Tom, there are," said the mayor.

"It's the Mice Wars," said Mr. Penny. He shook his head. "We lose a few people every year."

Suddenly the Littles realized there were many eyes looking at them from the windows of the building.

"This is where Major Nick's special friends live," Mayor Clutter said.

Children walked slowly out of the building. They circled the Littles, looking at them.

"Do you mean *all* of these children are Nick's friends?" said Mr. Little.

Mayor Clutter laughed. "Major Nick used to come here often," he said. "Talking to the children calmed him down after a bad battle with the mice. He had no children of his own, of course, but he had two special friends here."

At this point Mayor Clutter reached out and took the hands of a boy and a girl, each about ten years old.

"Major Nick found these two when they were babies," said Mayor Clutter. "He found them somewhere out in Mouse Country. No one knows who their parents were. The major was very fond of them. I want you to meet the McDust twins, Tip and Winkie."

Tip and Winkie McDust crossed their arms and shook hands with the Littles.

"Is old Major Nick hurt real bad?" asked Winkie.

"Is he?" Tip asked.

Mr. Little put his arms around the twins. "Major Nick wants to see you two," he said. "He was hurt in an accident with a cat. His sister is a nurse, and she's taking very good care of him."

Mr. Little smiled. "I'm sure that bringing you to visit him this Christmas will be the best thing we can do for Major Nick."

The next day at noon the snow stopped. As soon as it did, Uncle Pete went to the roof of the Biggs's house. He knew that Cousin Dinky would be flying again.

In about half an hour Uncle Pete saw the blue-and-white glider. It was making its way toward the house from the east.

Cousin Dinky was flying low, weaving his way under and over the trees.

A brisk wind carried the glider up a long curve to the roof. At the roof's edge two parachutes snapped open behind the aircraft. They were attached to it and acted like a brake to slow it down.

At the same time the tiny pilot threw out a fishhook anchor tied to a piece of string. The glider skidded to a safe landing on the roof. The fishhook anchor caught on a shingle, and held the glider fast.

Cousin Dinky and his wife, Della, climbed from the cockpit. Uncle Pete came across the roof to them.

Cousin Dinky said: "Uncle Pete— what's the news?"

Later, everyone was gathered in the living room. Plans were being made.

"The way I see it," Cousin Dinky said, "it will take *two* planes to get everyone back from Trash City."

"Why not make two trips then, Dinky?" asked Granny Little.

"I know the place," said Cousin Dinky. "I deliver the mail there once a week. Of course I do it without landing. There is a place to land but it would be hard to take off. There's so much junk all around."

"Then why would you want two planes?" asked Uncle Pete. "What good would that be?"

"I think I know what Dinky is going to suggest," said Della. She winked at her husband.

"Then you agree?" Cousin Dinky asked her.

"Of course," Della said. "It's a smashing plan."

Granny Little was all smiles. "Isn't that wonderful," she said. "They understand each other without talking."

"Well, how about telling the rest of us!" snapped Uncle Pete.

"We'll need to borrow Henry Biggs's gas-model airplane," Cousin Dinky said.

"That's easy enough to do," said Granny. "You did that once before."

"Yes, but it means we can't get going right away," Cousin Dinky went on. "We'll have to borrow the plane at night and get it back before Henry wakes up."

"We'll need the rest of today anyway," Della said, "to attach a pickup device to the glider."

"Will you get to the point, you two?" said Uncle Pete. "How are you going to pick anyone up if you can't take off from the town dump?"

"I'll *tow* the glider in back of Henry's model airplane," said Cousin Dinky. "Della will pilot the glider. When we get to the dump she'll release the glider and land it."

Della nodded, smiling. "Nifty!" she said.

"As soon as everyone is loaded aboard the glider," said Cousin Dinky, "I'll pick it up."

"*Pick it up?*" said Uncle Pete.

Using his hands to show how it could be done, the tiny pilot said: "I'll swoop down in the gas plane like this, trailing my fishhook anchor. As I come in over the glider the hook will catch on the pick-up device, pulling the glider into the air."

"Bravo!" said Della.

It was early Friday morning. Streaks of light showed in the eastern sky over the town dump. The noisy engine of Henry Bigg's gas-model airplane broke the silence.

Cousin Dinky was flying back and forth over the place where Della had landed the glider. That was some time ago. The tiny pilot was worried. He hoped Della was all right. He wondered if his directions to Trash City were correct. Was something changed so that she couldn't find the place? Why didn't she show up with the others? How much longer could the plane's supply of gasoline last?

For the fifteenth time Cousin Dinky dived down toward the parked glider. The fishhook anchor trailed out behind and below the airplane. He was practicing for the time he would lift the glider off the ground.

As Cousin Dinky practiced, he was careful not to catch the hook on the pick-up device he had built onto the glider. He came closer and closer each time. Finally he was satisfied that he knew just how to do it. Now—if only they would come.

Cousin Dinky glanced at the blue-and-white-glider below. He smiled to himself. Della had made a perfect landing on an old ironing board. Then she turned the craft around so that it faced the long runway of the ironing board. Everything worked just as they had planned.

There was a movement in the trash below!

Cousin Dinky flew the plane in low for a closer look.

A cat!

A huge, yellow cat was prowling around on the piles of trash. Its face was crisscrossed with scars. Spots of fur were missing from its coat.

The plane roared overhead. The cat spun around watching it closely. Cousin Dinky thought it was the meanest-looking animal he had ever seen.

Now—suddenly—there were the tiny people. They were a short distance from the cat. Della was leading the group. When she saw the airplane she waved.

"She doesn't see the cat," thought Cousin Dinky. He pointed toward the danger, but Della didn't seem to understand.

Dinky banked the airplane steeply. He roared in over the cat's head. The animal leaped at the plane, trying to bat it down.

Cousin Dinky saw that his friends were running toward the glider. At last they saw the danger. If Cousin Dinky could keep the cat's attention, they would have time to get aboard.

He pointed the nose of the airplane up. The airplane climbed steeply. Then, high in the sky, he dived toward the cat. At the very last second Cousin Dinky pulled out of the dive. The plane zoomed over the big cat's outstretched paws.

By this time Della and the others were climbing aboard the glider. Two of them were clinging to the wings. There wasn't enough room for everyone in the cockpit.

The cat was creeping slowly toward the tiny people in the glider. Suddenly he ran at them.

Now Cousin Dinky turned from the cat. He gunned the engine of the tiny craft, and raced away from the glider. He needed room to come in for the pickup. At the far end of the dump he banked steeply, and turned toward the ironing board.

The plane came in low toward the target. The fishhook anchor trailed out below and behind. Cousin Dinky knew he would have only one chance to pick up the glider.

Cousin Dinky kept one hand on the controls of the airplane. With the other hand he reached down between his feet. He picked up a dart he had gotten from Henry Bigg's dart game. The dart was made of metal with feathers on the end. It was heavy. The tiny pilot struggled to lift it over the edge of the cockpit. At last he got it into position.

Cousin Dinky dropped the dart.

ZZzzzingg!!

MMMEEOOOOOOooooow! The cat leaped into the air clawing at its tail.

The model airplane came in over the glider. The fishhook anchor hit the pick-up device squarely in the middle.

The glider was pulled down the ironing board runway and into the air.

"We did it!" yelled Cousin Dinky. From behind him he heard Della's cry above the roar of the engine:

"Fantastic!"

It was two o'clock Christmas morning. The Biggs and their visiting relatives were asleep. Near the Christmas tree in the Biggs's living room stood a doll house. It was a present from Mrs. Bigg to her niece, Mary.

At the moment the doll house was the scene of a Christmas party. All of the Littles were gathered there. Tiny lamps lighted the rooms. In the living room of the doll house stood a toy Christmas tree. There were presents under the tree. Wrapping paper was scattered about the floor.

Near the tiny tree, and lying on a miniature couch, was Uncle Nick. His friends, Tip and Winkie McDust, sat near him. They were laughing. Uncle Nick was smiling.

"Are you sure you'll be all right here?" asked Uncle Pete. He spoke to Uncle Nick.

"Don't worry about me, Peter," said Uncle Nick. "Enjoy the party." Then: "Let's open some more presents."

"What a wonderful idea Nick had," said Granny Little. "Using the doll house for a party."

"It's our only chance to see the doll house Mrs. Bigg made," said Mrs. Little. "Her niece will be taking it home with her when she leaves."

Just then Aunt Lily came in. She was carrying some of her fruitcake. "More goodies for the good people," she said. "The eggnog is coming right up."

Lucy picked up a present from under the tree. "It's for you, Tom," she said. "From Uncle Nick."

"Oh, wow!" Tom said. "I can hardly wait to open it. Uncle Nick gives super presents."

In a few moments the boy removed the wrapping from the present.

"It's Uncle Nick's *sword*!" said Tom. He ran to Uncle Nick, who looked startled.

"Is something wrong, Uncle Nick?" asked Tom.

"Nick—you gave Tom your sword!" said Uncle Pete. "What on earth for? You'll need it."

"Well, I ... I ..." stammered Uncle Nick.

"Oh my stars!" said Aunt Lily. She covered her face with her hands. "What have I done?"

Everyone turned to Aunt Lily.

"Tom," said Aunt Lily, "I wrapped up that present for you when your uncle thought he was going to die. Nick *insisted* that he wanted to leave you his sword. Now, of course, he ..."

"Oh." Tom looked disappointed.

" ... and I forgot to unwrap it after he decided to go on living a little longer," Aunt Lily went on. "I'm sorry."

"That's okay," Tom said. "I ... I understand." He held out the sword to Uncle Nick.

"No, Tom — no!" said Uncle Nick. "I really want you to have it. I just decided. I really do."

"Golly," said Tom. "Wow! This is the best present I ever had." He looked the sword over.

"Nick," said Granny Little. "That was sweet."

Uncle Nick laughed. "Guess what!" he said. "I just discovered it's more fun to give things away while you're still around." He smiled at everyone. "You know — it's great to be alive!"

"That reminds me of a song," said Cousin Dinky. He grinned as he reached for his guitar.

"Oh no!" said Uncle Pete under his breath. "Dinky's going to ruin the party."

(Cousin Dinky loved to sing. He wrote songs about his adventures. The trouble was he had a terrible singing voice. Only Granny Little, who was hard of hearing, liked to hear Cousin Dinky sing.)

"Oh good!" said Granny Little. "Quiet, everyone! I want to hear every word."

Cousin Dinky sat on a stool, strummed his guitar, and sang:

It's great to be alive!
When I'm flying through the skies
Thinking I may crash
In a city made of trash
It's *great* to be alive!

On other sorts of days
In other kinds of ways
When I'm all alone and still
And suddenly my heart fills
with—*It's great to be alive!*

And when Christmas Day is come
And here is everyone
My family and my friends
May the story never end
It's *great* to be alive!

"Why, Dinky," said Della, "I never heard that song before. You made it up just now."

"I like it," Uncle Nick said. "Especially that line: 'It's great to be alive!'"

Tom tapped Uncle Pete on the shoulder. "Okay, Uncle Pete," he said. "The song is over. You can take your fingers out of your ears now."